Tales
From The
Purple Penguin

Charles Huckelbury

BleakHouse Publishing

2008

Tales From The Purple Penguin

Poems by

Charles Huckelbury

Cover Art:
Sara Rubenson

Cover Design:
Kyoko Wakamatsu

Copyright © 2008 by Charles Huckelbury

ISBN-13: 978-0-9797065-4-7
ISBN-10: 0-9797065-4-8

BleakHouse Publishing
NEC Box 67
New England College
Henniker, New Hampshire 03242
www.BleakHousePublishing.com

Dedication

For Barry Roth, teacher, mentor, friend, and the first person to convince me that you don't have to be a sissy to read or write poetry.

Acknowledgements

I owe so much to so many; here are but a few: my parents, Jane and Charlie, who began bringing me books very early and never stopped; my wife, Susan, educator, author, partner, and best friend, who makes all things possible; Rob Johnson for having the courage to take on this project; and all the help, hustlers and hapless people from forty years ago who still populate my memory and served as inspiration for the characters and events in these poems.

Table of Contents

The Help

The Hustlers

The Hapless

The Help

Genesis

Big David sat on
two-thirds of the couch
while I stood by the door.

Hank put his feet up
on the desk and looked at me.
"L. D. and B. D.?

"That's us."

"What's that stand for?"

"Little David and Big David."

"No last names?"

"That's us," I repeated.

"I need something for taxes,"

We both stared at him for
twenty seconds until I
helped him out.

"Cash. No checks. No taxes.
You pay the lawyer if we get busted.
You pay the bondsman if we go to jail.
You pay the doctors if we're shot or cut."

He chewed his lip.
"I don't expect that kind
of trouble."

"We know."

"I've already
 hired four other bouncers
 to help you."

"Fire them."

"All of them?"

"All of them."

He sat up and looked at
both of us again. "And
you'll be enough?"

"We'll be all you need."

"You're sure?"

We looked at each other
and laughed.

Just like we did
every time.

The Christening

We were stuck for a name for the
new joint when

Pete got screaming drunk on
purple Jesus and

puked all over Harold's spiffy
white tux.

Annie wouldn't let him go to the car
for his gun,

so he waddled over to the bathroom
to clean up.

Mayalee laughed and said he looked like a
purple penguin.

Pete looked up from his spot
under the table.

"That's it," he said.
And it was.

Rock and Roll

The house band was
two guitars and a drum kit,
all for three twenty-five a week.
I guess the lead singer got
the extra twenty-five bucks.
The only songs they could play were
three by Jimi Hendrix.

But they played loud,
which covered the noise when the
fights broke out. By the time
we opened at midnight, most of
the customers were
too drunk to notice.

Fashion Statement

I didn't usually work in places where
customers wore
>   ties or
>   sport coats or
>   jewelry.

I worked in places that required me to
hurt certain customers
who usually wore knives or
guns instead,

like one Saturday night when two guys were
sitting on Eleanor's Mustang when she
came out and looked easy.

When she told Pete later that she had never
seen anyone pull a gun that fast, I felt
like Jesse goddamn James. I just knew
I was her hero.

And that's why my feelings were
almost hurt when
I walked into the
leather-padded,
wingtip-catering
place she ran to fill in for her bartender.

She took one look at me and said,
"Oh no. Anyone but you."

The Worst Insult

I was called a lot of things
at the Penguin, but the

worst was when I knocked out
a guy for trying to crash the door

for the third time. When his head
hit the pavement, someone in

line waiting to get in said,
"He acts just like a cop."

Domestic Abuse

White knights don't wear khakis
and cowboy boots, but when the dirtbag in
the pickup tried to pull the blonde

into his truck, I rode to the rescue. He
had her almost in when I got to his door.
She was still screaming for help

so I told him once to let her go.
He held on and told me to
mind my own business.

But rescuing damsels and
slaying dragons *was* my business, and
business was good, which made him

let go of her and bleed.
She stopped screaming and
pulled out a Kleenex and

called him "Baby" and wiped
most of the blood off his face.
Then she stared at me and

called me an asshole for
hurting her husband.

I went back inside,
took off my white hat,
and burned it.

Diplomatic Immunity

I had a drunk pinned in a
wrist lock on the way
out the front door when
Hank walked in with Kate.

Hank said, "Don't hurt him."

When the Penguin first opened,
he told us
not to do what we did at his
old bar across town. This was a
new place where people could drink without
stitches or broken bones.

But thugs don't stop being thugs
just because the wallpaper's different.

Hank said, "Easy with him."

He patted the drunk on the shoulder,
like they were fraternity brothers
exchanging a secret sign.

Hank said, "Get a little air and come back later."

The drunk squinted and tried to focus on Hank's
professional smile. He wobbled a little and then
spat right in his face. I cranked the wrist lock
a little tighter and brought him
up on his toes while we waited.

Hank said, "Take him out back and kill him."

Blind

Sherry always
took off her glasses
when she was
on stage, not
because she was
prettier without them
but so she couldn't
see the drunks
drooling over her body
while she danced to *Bitch*
by the Rolling Stones.

Career Change

Hindu was a bartender
who wanted to be a
bouncer until the night of the
big biker brawl.

The ER nurse had to
shave half of his beard to
put the stitches in.

Then Hindu wanted to be a
bartender again.

Clueless

Standing outside the Penguin, I gave everyone
heading through the door a quick exam. I let most
walk on by me,

but a few drunks and winos who
banged against the walls like a three-cushion
pool shot didn't.

Usually all I needed to do was point in the
opposite direction and they got the idea. I was
famous along the strip.
I was The Man.

A few others flunked the test if they were
dressed too well or weren't redneck enough. I
never turned anyone away for being stupid
if they were too drunk to know it.

Migraine Remedy

The woman in the long dress kept
hitting me over the head with a cane and screaming like I had
just run over

her poodle. Every shot felt like
she had thrown a rock at me, and I knew
my head would be sore in the

morning when I stepped under the shower.
But it was the screaming that finally
got to me, so I stopped

punching her boyfriend
sitting on the floor in front of me.

Odalisque

Brenda had never worked topless before, but
on New Year's Eve, one of the other girls OD'ed
and another was in jail for setting her boyfriend's
crotch on fire while he was driving her to the
bus station. It took Pete maybe ten seconds
and twenty bucks to convince Brenda to strip.

She didn't have a regular costume, so she just
pulled off her sweatshirt and
stepped out of her jeans and
was ready to go.

Underneath were black steroid panties that
should have had a Packers logo on them.
Stretch marks streaked in four directions like
the interstate highway system, but farther
north, Brenda gave topless a new meaning.

Ten minutes later, a guy at the bar offered
her double Pete's money to put her
clothes back on.

All Major Credit Cards Accepted

We didn't take plastic
on the way in

but once the suckers were
drunk or bleeding

we took plastic
on the way out

along with everything else
in their wallets.

Equal Opportunity

I knocked out a black guy
who wanted to be a gangster.

Then a white guy said I had
punched him just because he was black.

So I knocked him out just to show I wasn't a
racist redneck.

Just a redneck.

Shell Game

Walking out of the Penguin a little
before 3:00 in the morning, I was
the baddest bouncer in the
baddest bar in the city.

In the empty parking lot, I stood
like Leonidas before the Persians,
confident, capable, and comforted
by the weight of my guns,

trying to see stars above me but
blinded by the mercury lights that
didn't keep the thieves and hustlers away.

I walked to my car, gun hand free,
daring anyone to fuck with me if they
were crazy enough to try to stop me
from going home again to an empty bed.

Home Run

The bones of my left hand weren't as
thick as the head of the guy I hit, so
I went to work the next night with
plaster up to my elbow.

Pete gave me a spring-loaded sap
for the suckers, but I didn't have
the touch. I hit the first guy like Hank Aaron had hit number
755

By the time he got to x-ray,
the sap was out of my pocket,
wiped clean, and back
into Pete's desk.

Ambushed

Big David yelled in my ear that
someone wanted to see me at the door,
probably some drunk I had turned away
earlier begging for another chance.

I should have known better,
but it was late.

The doorman buzzed me through
the first door, and I pushed open the
steel door that led to clean air.

"Hey David." The bastard
fired as soon as I turned his way.

He was at the top of the stairs on his
belly with a rifle, that turned out to be a
single-shot .22. Lucky for me he only
had one bullet that I barely felt.

He hauled ass before I could shoot him.
But at least I got his gun.

The Invisible Hand

The Saturday night crowd
was down to half,
a lot of dancers but just
a few drinkers.

Pete ate a black beauty and
chased it with Crown Royal. It
was only 9:00 but he was already
midnight mean.

"That new place over on Central is killing us."
I nodded.

"Be nice if we were full again."
I nodded.

"Hard to do with that new place open."
I nodded.

Pete took another sip of Crown Royal.

"Burn it."
I did.

Big Little Horn

I should have minded my own business,
but Dee came out of the Penguin
just as I pulled to the curb and asked me to
walk around back with him because he had
some trouble with some not-from-Cleveland
Indians, but before we got there, a '64 Chevy
bounced out of the alley and blocked the
sidewalk, and I knew what Custer must have
felt like looking at all those Indians because there
were at least a hundred in the car, and they were
all screaming, and they all had guns, and
they were all pointed at me, and the son of a
bitch who had talked me into this shit took one
look and asked me if I had my gun, and I had to
tell him I didn't and I asked if he had his, but he
didn't either, so I said, "Let's go," and we started
to turn when all those Indians started shooting
at us, which made us run that much faster until
I got to the corner of the building just as a bullet
chipped brick six inches from my head, which
helped me jump over a goddamn Buick parked
at the curb and not stop until I got to the
Waffle House one block over.

Witchy Woman

No one ever knew why but every time
"Witchy Woman" hit the juke, Tina

started pulling off her clothes, even when
it wasn't her time to dance. Maybe that's

why she exploded the night I knocked out
a couple of guys with more balls than

brains. Her song came on and she was in the
middle of peeling off her panties when it started.

The big one bled a lot, and Tina
ran up to me naked and begged me not to

hit him again. I didn't, and it had nothing to do
with Tina being naked.

After we cleaned the place up, she ran into
Pete's office and told him that she couldn't take

it any more. She gave him a going away
blowjob and then came out to the bar for

a last drink. She sipped straight gin and told
me what an uncivilized animal I was.

The Hustlers

Ethology

Like lions to a Serengeti watering hole
they migrated to
the Penguin,

searching with their flat
shining eyes for
        the weak
                the lame
                        the stupid
                                the drunk

or

celebrating a recent score
and leaving behind
        the poor
                the hurt
                        the scared
                                the dead.

They hunted in packs,
in teams, or
alone, and

during a drought, when
prey were scarce,
they ate each other.

Fred

There's something unsettling
about having another man
touch your ass
when you're straight
and your boss has
just decided to
change a cowboy bar
into a gay bar and
you've never worked in
one of those before and
you don't know how to act
and you don't know how the hell
you ever got into that spot in
the first place and you don't know
why they even need a
leg breaker anyway
when nobody ever fights
but the girls.

Damage Control

The third time I threw
the guy out, I finally saw how
he was getting in through the
fire exit. That's when I put
my hands on him.

He tumbled across the carpet
in the foyer, came up cat quick,
and pulled a box cutter from
his boot. He dropped into a
crouch like he knew what he
was doing, so I pulled the .45
and pointed it at his head.

He looked at the gun
then at his knife. He
looked at the gun again
and back at his knife.

He stood up and closed the cutter.
"Will you do me a favor and
hold this for me before
I hurt myself?"

Bobby's Big Surprise

Bobby was a wanabe from
out of town. Danny DeVito with a flash
roll, he lit up everybody's radar the second
he walked in. Before I could give him

a bump frisk, Trixie was after him like a
barracuda on a minnow. With her hand
on his prick, Bobby's glasses steamed
up so fast he was hooked before I put

the second round in front of them. Ten
more minutes and they were in the rear
booth with Trixie's hands working
slicker than a booster in Wal-Mart. Five
minutes later, they were on the
way to the No Tell Motel down the street.

We saw Trixie the next night in a new dress
and wig with a Piaget knock-off on her
wrist. We didn't see Bobby again,
but Trixie told us how

they had gotten to the motel after she blew
him in the car and she had gone into the
bathroom to tidy up and come back out
with a hard-on that scared poor Bobby so
bad that he ran out of the room and never
missed the wallet she had clipped.

Faux Fighters

At least once a month I would
find someone standing against a
wall, usually with his arms folded
across his chest trying to look like
a bouncer, as if rolling around
on the floor in spilled beer
and cigarette butts was
glamorous.

I even had one of them give me
a warning when I asked him
what the fuck he was doing. He was
one of Star Baby's tricks, so I only
hurt him a little bit.

ZZ Topless

Pete explained glitter rock
so we were ready when
the first crowd showed up with
permed hair
eye shadow
sequined shirts and
glitter on their faces.
And these were the guys.

Acts of God

Earthquakes
Hurricanes
Tornados
Typhoons
Lightening
Hail
Tsunamis

and

Fires at bars with insurance
when the customers have
gone elsewhere.

Mistaken Identity

Geese mate for life, but Shirley and
Doug weren't geese, just two
hustlers trying to get over. Doug
bought the Dungeon and

gave it to Shirley to run and fuck
whoever she wanted, so she hired Larry
to play with and keep the rowdies
from breaking too much glass. She also

hired some working girls and always
got a piece of their action. But she didn't
tell Larry, so when he showed up the first
night and saw some guy in a suit with

his hand up a waitress's ass, he did the
bouncer thing and tossed the john out into
the snow. When he got back in, he expected
an MVP award, but what he got was Shirley

and the hooker both yelling at him. Shirley
grabbed him by the balls and pulled him
into her office. After she told him how
goddamn dumb he was, she pulled

up her skirt and bent over the desk and
made them both feel a lot better. Then she
made him go back outside and pay the hooker
twenty bucks for the trick he had bounced.

Retail Sales

Guns were common
at the Penguin,
even if we had a
sign that said only
the guys we knew
could carry them.

I carried one.
Sometimes two.
And a knife.

I also sold guns
at the Penguin. I sold the
same gun five times to
guys who kept leaving
it in their cars while
they were inside.

Payday

Two dope fiends sat in a corner booth,
wiping their noses and nursing straight
club sodas while they waited, watching the

off-duty rent-a-cop at the bar flash
his counterfeit Rolex again. Two more
Budweisers would send his bladder to the

bathroom, where the clean-up crew
would find him in the last stall,
bleeding and broke.

If Only

The drag queen was hustling the real
estate salesman for drinks and
promising a blowjob he wouldn't

ever forget because it was her time
of the month and she couldn't
fuck him. By his fourth double

Chivas, he believed he looked just
like Russell Crowe, so the first lie
went down easily.

The Greatest Story Ever Told

In the hallway by the bathroom
one of the working girls had her hand
down the Wal-Mart john's pants and
her tongue in his ear, swearing that she
had really, really never felt a bigger one.

That wasn't what his wife usually told him
after he came in twenty seconds, but on
Saturday night with half his paycheck
gone for champagne cocktails, it was
easy to believe.

Categorical Imperative

Everybody stole from
everybody else at the Penguin.
The bartenders did it.
The waitresses did it.
The strippers did it.
The hookers did it.
The bouncers and
the doorman did it.
Even the fat girl
            with the Mercedes did it.
I did it, too, but because
I liked the owners,
I stole less than anybody else.

The Surgeon General's Report

Sandy stripped and
hooked her way
across the city until she
had enough to buy
the Blue Note.

Thirty going on
eighty, she still danced
a little when she was high—
Kmart merchandise in a
Tiffany box.

Twice a week
she brought her
Mardis Gras makeup
and plastic tits
across the street
to hear our band
and hit on the help.

She strutted up to
Jake the Snake
after watching him KO
a smartass carny with
more tattoos than skill.

She stroked his fingers
under the bar towel
he had wrapped
around his hand and
took a big hit off a Kool.

Then she blew that shit
right into Jake's face like
Bette goddamn Davis.

Jake hated smokers, so
he grabbed Sandy by the
throat and stuffed the bloody
towel into her mouth.

Later he almost apologized.

A Rose by Any Other Name

"Hey, baby,"
said the gangster and
snapped his fingers.

"My name's Laurie,"
the bartender told him.

"Don't be such a cunt,"
the gangster replied.

When he woke up,
he sucked soup
for eight weeks
until his jaw healed.

Show and Don't Tell

The front row on Friday nights was always
filled with suits and ties from the office,

all expecting to see secretaries, nurses,
and teachers strip just for them.

What they got were hookers planted in the
audience and dressed for the part.

First prize was a hundred bucks, but the
girls also got a piece of the door money

the suckers had paid to see them on
amateur topless night.

Alone in a Crowd

Twice I warned the guy not to touch
        the girls. The third time I

knocked him down, but he jumped up
        and ran to a table with

four other guys. He stopped and
        pointed. "I'm with them."

One of the other guys looked
        at the bloody mouth,

then at me and said
        "Oh no he's not."

Money Talks

Pete called at 2:20 on my
night off, drunk and
mad because he had just lost
twelve hundred bucks
in liar's poker
to a guy we both hated.

The chump was about to
leave the Penguin and
walk into a cold, black
night where anything could happen.

I got there just as he
pulled out of the lot,
the winner's smile still
frozen on his face.
I cold trailed him to a
pancake house where

he was stupid enough to park in a
dark spot near a Dumpster. When
he came out,
full of boysenberry syrup and
bad luck,

I stepped up behind him as
he put the key in his car's door.

I met Pete for breakfast thirty minutes
later on the other side of town and tried to
give him his money back. He wouldn't take
it at first. He said it wasn't about the money,
but I knew better.

It was always about the money.

Indecent Proposal

"You've never had a
big girl before, have you?"
I stepped back a foot and
took another look at her.

Marcia was about 200 pounds
more than a big girl, and
she was right about the never
part of it. I shook my head.

"It'll blow your mind,"
she promised with a wink.
Getting an image of her
naked meant that my mind

was about the only thing
she would be able to blow
because nothing else was
going to cooperate.

No Refunds

They came in like four
castaways washed up after a
shipwreck.

Five pairs of eyes estimated
what the jewelry would bring.

Four legs left to check out
their car.

The first citizen looked at the
smashed pinball machine and
asked where he could hang his coat.

"Keep it on if you want
to leave with it."

The rest squinted through the smoke,
        exchanged looks, and
        turned around. They
        tried the door, but it
        locked automatically
        behind them.

Their eyes pleaded with me, so
I nodded to the doorman, who
buzzed them back out.

Twenty bucks for
sixty seconds.

Apologia Pro Vita Sua

It's a little past 3:00, too
early or late
for burgers if you
have to get up
in the morning.
But not for me or the
two guys with the girl
in the tight jeans.

All three are looking at me
while we wait until
one walks over with his
hands in his pocket.

"You know her?"
nodding toward the girl,
who tries not to look at me
but does anyway.

"No."
"You were looking
goddamn hard
at her."

I shrug and lift my head to
smell the onion rings coming
out of the Fryolater just as
a cop walks in.

We both look at him. The
guy looks back at me
and smiles.

"He can't stop it."

I smile back.
"I don't want him to."

Now he's looking at my hands
buried in my jacket pockets.
He licks his lips and glances
back toward the other two.
Then he slowly pulls his
empty hands from his pockets.

"Look, uh, I don't do this much, but
I'm sorry. Okay?"

I shrug again.
"Sure."

He tries to strut a little when he
walks back to the others.

My order comes out, and I
grab the sack and pay.
I pass close enough to brush
his shoulders as I leave.

Like two sharks,
we check each other out
and then go our
separate ways.

The Hapless

Disney World Without the Rides

They came through the door
thirsty for what was cold,
horny for what was hot, and
happy to be where they could get both.

They went home
smelling like a dirty ash tray,
wearing stupid-stitches in a fat lip, and
broke because all the girls were pros.

They woke up with
a head twice its size,
a mouth full of dirty socks, and
last night's beer on the pillow beside them.

They had so much fun that they
brought their friends the next night.

The Dance

"Watch it, David.
He's got a gun."

I already knew that because it
was pointed at my face and
close enough to grab if the
window had been down. We
stared at each other until he
started the car.

I got out of the way while he
backed out, wishing I had
something other than air in
my hand.

He kept the gun aimed at me
until he was in the middle of the lot, then
rolled down the window and
spit in my direction.

He was almost to the driveway
when Rusty eased up beside me and
 slipped a .38 into my hand. "Pete
said he didn't want it back
if you shoot him."

I thought about it. He was still
close enough, but Candy's place
was just across the street and she had
already replaced the front window
once that week when I missed.

Rained Out

I let her in free
every night, but when
I asked her out, she
shivered and
shook her head.

I asked Rusty to
find out why, but that
part was easy. She had
seen me work. Maybe she
just needed to see my
funny side.

So the next night I
sat down at her table,
ignored her date, and
told her that if she
didn't have breakfast
with me I would
send her boyfriend to the
emergency room.

She didn't laugh,
she cried, and I kept
eating breakfast alone.

What Goes Around

George was a bounty hunter for a
local bondsman, and he carried
a .44 magnum because Clint Eastwood did
and looked cool.

But George wasn't cool.

He had yanked a couple
of guys out of the Penguin for
minor cases, and one of them
knew some people
who weren't too happy about it

because the guy did some things for them
that nobody else would do, and with
him in jail, they had to find some other gofer
to run their coke up from Miami.

So they decided to blow George's ass off for
busting their guy and
walking around like
he was bullet proof and
muscling people who wouldn't fight
but mostly because
he just needed his ass blown off.

Which was a hell of a project,
since George's ass
was so big he couldn't reach around it.
Which is why he
didn't wear any underwear and
why he had to rinse off in the shower
after every shit.

Which is why he usually
got naked before he sat down
and got comfortable.

Which is how the cops
found him after his girlfriend
called to report that someone
had put three loads of number one

buckshot into him
while he was on the can
reading an old *Hustler* magazine.

A-Listed

Two tuxedos and
two gowns
unassed a red Lincoln
just past midnight.

They looked like money
but bitched
about the cover charge.
When one
sucker punched me,

we all ended up in a big pile
just outside the door,
the men bleeding and
the women screaming.

I finally let the guys
crawl back to the Lincoln.

One of the women
gave me the finger
after they were inside
with the doors locked.

Subterranean

Crouched
in the dark
and the dirt
and the grease,
he looked like a mole,
nose twitching and squinty eyes staring at me.

With his arms and
legs wrapped
around the Ford's
undercarriage,
I couldn't
pull him out, and he
wouldn't come
on his own,
even after
I put away the knife.

Unconditional Surrender

Slumped on the floor
in a puddle of puke,
he had one hand wrist deep in
piss when I pushed open the
stall door to see if he was
still alive.

His other arm was tied off
with the spike still buried. When
he lifted his head and
coughed, a yellow-green string
dribbled down his chin
and dropped on to his shirt.

He spit once and said,
"Man, that's good shit."

Then his head sagged until
his face rested on the dirty
toilet seat again.

Oops

Three real estate salesmen
sat in the second booth arguing after their third round until I
walked over and
asked them to hold it down.

Bob waved me off like a second-grade student.
Fuck you, he said.

I slapped the drink
out of his hand,
then slapped him.
Everyone shut up. Bob
wiped blood
from his mouth
with a paper napkin
and told me he had
a gun in his car.

I pulled up my sweater and showed him the .45.
Bet mine's bigger, I said.
And a lot closer.

Threat Assessment

The man who
threatened to kill me
sat on the ground
by his van
holding his head.

He didn't hear me
until I was
five feet away.
By then,
all he could see
was gun.

You the one
wants to shoot me?

His head
hit the door
when he jerked
it back.

I was just mad
because you
hurt my jaw.

He looked
at the .45.
I don't even
have a gun.

I nodded.
Wait here and
I'll go
get you one.

I was nearly
at the door
when I
heard the van
spit gravel
on the way
out of the parking lot.

Once

Big David never thought much of small
guns. He said you always had to shoot
the guy more than once. For him,
bigger was always better, so
when Sonny nearly died after getting shot
once with a .25, BD was so surprised he
bought one as a backup.

Then he went home one weekend and
gave the gun to his dad, who said
he needed something for protection.

The next day, his dad shot himself
in the head. That time once was enough.

Georgia on My Mind

The redneck came in close to midnight and saw Dennis on
stage

with three white strippers and

didn't like it because Dennis was
the only thing black in the whole

joint, so the redneck pulled a knife
on him, but Candy saw it and told

me and pointed the guy out right up
close to the stage where Dennis

was singing "Knock on Wood,"
so I stepped up to the stage when the girls

did their bump and grind and whispered to Dennis to sing
loud, and he turned

to the band and pumped his arm twice while the redneck and I
danced until

I got his knife and made sure it didn't go to the emergency
room with him

and fall out and hurt the nurse who
was putting his face back together.

Upscale Gunfight

I had never been shot at
from a Cadillac before,
especially by people
wearing good clothes,
but by the time we were
finished rolling around
in the mud and sand
in the parking lot,
they didn't look so nice any more.

Larry said they
must have stolen
the clothes, the jewelry, and
the Caddy because they sure
acted like a bunch
of thugs, but I could tell
they weren't really
serious about it.

They only got off
one shot.

The Biker Who Went Boom

If he hadn't taken things so personally
he wouldn't have ended up on his back
in the alley behind the Penguin
with a hole in his chest.

But he had a gun and something
to prove to his partner.

Which is why brains are better than a .38
and a load of testosterone, because you
never know when you'll meet someone
with a .45 already out and working.

Minuet in D-Minor

Drunks always think they are
        faster, tougher, meaner,
so when the guy in the plaid jacket
        hit me with his best shot,

he just knew that I would fall
        down, like the cowboys in all
those John Wayne movies.
        When I didn't, he said,

"Can we talk about this?"

We did.
Oh yes we did.

It Ain't Kansas, Toto

Jerry got loud on too many
Black Russians one night and
told me not to fuck with him
when I asked him to keep it down.

Jerry sold cars for a living.
I sent people to the emergency room.

He was a fat forty.
I was a tight twenty-three.

While he was having his morning coffee,
I was running five miles.

While he was showing cars,
I was in the gym sparring.

His last fight had been in the sixth grade.
Mine had been that morning.

So I
sat down across from him in
the booth and told him what
he would look like when he saw
his first customer the next day.

Jerry stared through the vodka
and apologized.

Most weren't
that easy.

Dishonorable Discharge

Mike got discharged and
bought a bar down the street
from the Penguin. Maybe
the Air Force doesn't
make guys run or do PT,
because you could
have drilled three holes in
him and rolled a strike every time.

His pistol was parked over
his zipper, which is the only
place he could reach, and he
had a nasty habit of not paying
his girls on time.

When Alicia didn't get her
money the second week
her boyfriend got his
crew together and paid Mike's
apartment a visit while he
was tending bar. They sold

most of the furniture and all
the booze, but the clothes
wouldn't fit any of them, so
they piled them up in
the living room and set them on
fire.

Parole Violation

I knew
the guy was drunk when I
let him in, but it was a slow night
and we needed the money. Five
minutes later, another guy came
up and told me a drunk was
bothering him and his daughter.

It's the
same drunk, so I walked
over to the table and
told him he's gotta leave.

I just
got out of prison,
he said, like that's
a pass to bother people. I let him know
I didn't care, and he tried
a sucker move
that was too old and too slow.

I felt
the punch all the way to
my shoulder, and he tumbled
over sideways onto the carpet.

After I
had taken out the garbage, I came back
in and offered to buy the guy and his
daughter a drink. Funny thing, they headed
out the door in a trot, the father holding
the daughter's arm and
both looking back like
the devil was chasing them.

We had
a lot of ungrateful people like that.

Christmas Dinner

Two chili dogs and
fries at the
Weiner King.

Four kids serving
      a wino
      a hooker
      a dope-sick junkie
      and me.

On my way out, the kid
behind the counter
turns up the radio
that plays
"Joy to the World."

Only the good

I owed Star Baby a breakfast at
a 24-hour Greek joint and then
a ride home. She's the
only one I've ever seen
who could eat
lamb in tomato sauce
at 3:30 in the morning.

The Ford rolled up and
blocked me just as
we pulled to the
end of the drive.

They were good but not
quite good enough. When
the back window slid down,
I pulled Star Baby into the
seat and fell on top of her.

The shotgun blew out the
windshield and spread shattered
glass over us like jagged hail
stones. When I heard the
Ford's engine rev, I peeked
over the dash.

Star Baby sat up and
brushed glass out of her hair.
She looked out through
the hole and then reached
for the door.

"I think I'll call a cab from here."

Menage a trios

The asshole just wouldn't
stop throwing ice at the band,
and even though I knew how
bad they were, it was my job
to stop that kind of shit.

I told him twice, but
he wouldn't quit, so the third time
I went over to the table and
punched him on his
sweet spot.

While his friends
were getting him up
and out of the place, his
date slid up to me and
asked me to buy her
breakfast before we
went to the Holiday Inn.

A Knife in the Hand is Worth Two in the Back

When he paid the cover,
the biker said that
we had sent his friend home
bloody the night before.

Becky sent Star Baby to finger
the guy, and ten minutes later,
one of the waitresses told me
someone was passed out.

When I walked back to the
big bar, it was the same guy
face down on the table.

I nudged his shoulder, and his
head came up,
too quick for a drunk,
and his eyes were clear.

I pointed toward the door.
"You gotta go."

He got up and pushed the chair back.
"You first."

Like I just fell off the turnip truck.
"Not a chance."

I got a position on him
and waited. Finally
he moved ahead of me, but
as soon as we got into the
darkest part of the club,
he spun. The knife
glittered for a second when
the strobe hit it.

I caught the blade in the
webbing of my right hand,
closed my fist on it, and
beat the living shit out of his
face and head with
the sap I had in the other hand.

Pete gave me the
rest of the night off to
get stitched up, but at least
I rode to the ER in a car
instead of an ambulance.

Requiem

Forty years after getting three plays
for a quarter on the jukebox, I let
my wife's younger son touch a scar
on my neck.

"What's that from?"

"Surgery," I said.
With a broken Budweiser bottle.

The older son pointed to a white
crescent over my right eye.

"What about that one?"

"More surgery," I told him.
With a pewter ring.

His girlfriend giggled once and
covered her mouth.
"Your nose looks funny."

"More surgery," I said.
From a pool cue.

The blood has dried, the bones
have knitted, but the January ache
reminds me of how stupid I was,

an armchair gladiator with an empty
suitcase where my memories should be.

About the Author

Charles Huckelbury is the recipient of four PEN American awards for fiction and non-fiction. He is a regular contributor and a member of the editorial board of the *Journal of Prisoners on Prison*, an academic journal published by the University of Ottawa and devoted to criminal justice issues. He also writes a monthly op-ed column for the *Concord Monitor*. His poetry has been published in the *Northern New England Review* and his fiction most recently in *Exiled Voices, Portals of Discovery* (New England College Press, 2008). Huckelbury is a member of the board of directors of New Hampshire Pathways to Hope, a non-profit group for which he trains service dogs to assist the disabled. Charles Huckelbury is in the 34th consecutive year of a life sentence at the New Hampshire State Prison in Concord.

About the Artists

Sara Rubenson (*Cover Art*) is studying art at the University of Massachusetts in Boston. She has worked on art projects for *Tacenda Literacy Magazine* and BleakHouse Publishing.

Kyoko Wakamatsu (*Cover Design*) graduated from University of Delaware with a degree in Apparel Design. She was a finalist in the U.S. Arts of Fashion Competition and her work was exhibited at Le Concours International des Jeunes in Paris, France, as one of 10 U.S. representatives for 2002-2003. Since graduation, Wakamatsu has worked in various creative fields, including interior design, advertisement design, and fashion design.